Mimi, the Solo Magician Mom, and CAMERON

A Donor Conception Story

Written by Melissa A. Macdonald

Illustrated by Jupiter's Muse

Mimi, the Solo Magician Mom, and Cameron
Copyright © 2022 by Melissa A. Macdonald

All rights reserved. No part of this publication may be reproduced, distributed, or transmitted in any form or by any means, including photocopying, recording, or other electronic or mechanical methods, without the prior written permission of the author, except in the case of brief quotations embodied in critical reviews and certain other non-commercial uses permitted by copyright law.

Tellwell Talent
www.tellwell.ca

ISBN
978-0-2288-6046-4 (Hardcover)
978-0-2288-6045-7 (Paperback)

For Aidan. You will always be my most miraculous choice.

To all of the Single Parents by Choice before me and to the mothers who shared their journeys of perseverance and strength. For those who are still thinking and trying, I assure you that the biggest regret is not trying at all.

Special thanks to my nieces Abigail and Amelia for asking difficult questions, and to my family and friends for their unconditional love and support.

Last but not least, to sperm, egg and embryo donors for giving families the opportunity to make their parenting dreams a reality. Your generosity creates tiny humans who bring more love into this world than you may ever realize.

Hi. I'm Cameron and these are my friends. We are in Grade 2 at Stoney Field Elementary School.

His name is Edgar and he lives at our zoo.
People come from all over just to see this.

Magician

Edgar always gets ice cream too. He's the only elephant I know that likes it as much as we do.

Mom has her own way of doing almost everything. In fact, she never uses a recipe. She just throws whatever's in the fridge into a pot.

Mom says that she always dreamed of starting a family. In fact, she wanted me so badly that she travelled to the ends of the earth to find a way to bring me into her life.

When she returned empty-handed, she checked her big book of magic and still couldn't find a way to make a baby all on her own. That's when she knew she needed to ask for help.

Mom found other people who also chose to have children on their own, and she listened carefully when they told her how they became parents. Although no two stories seemed to be exactly the same, they had some important things in common.

An egg from a woman and some sperm from a man are combined to create what's called an embryo. Then a woman grows that embryo in her uterus until it becomes a baby.

Since Mom already had an egg and was able to grow an embryo, she needed to find a sperm donor to help.

Spoiler Alert!

Mom did an amazing job growing that embryo into what's called a fetus, and after nearly 40 weeks it was a full-sized baby who turned out to be me!

On Valentine's Day, I was born with two locks of hair and lungs that were made for singing.

Out of this world, right?

My family is made up of Mom, me, our cat Abracadabra, and, of course, a couple of white bunny rabbits.

Edgar joins us on special holidays.

While families may not look the same on the outside, on the inside I hope they feel as much love for one another as we do.

Discussion Questions

What is special about Cameron's family?

Who is part of your family?

How do you think your family is unique?

What makes you feel most proud to be part of your family?

About the Author

Melissa A. Macdonald is a Solo Mother by Choice (SMBC) by way of donor conception. After three years and several assisted reproductive procedures, in 2018, at the age of 42, Melissa was blessed with the birth of her son Aidan.

Melissa and Aidan live in Hamilton, Ontario, Canada. They enjoy exploring waterfalls, riding trains and making smoothies together.

Made in United States
North Haven, CT
10 September 2023